THE WHEELS ON THE BUS

ON THE BUS

GO

ROUND AND ROUND

AND OTHER

ACTION NURSERY RHYMES

Published by Bonney Press,
an imprint of Hinkler Books Pty Ltd
45–55 Fairchild Street
Heatherton Victoria 3202 Australia
www.hinkler.com.au

BONNEY
PRESS

© Hinkler Books Pty Ltd 2015, 2016

Illustrators: Steph Baxter, Sarah Coleman, Jon Contino, Sarah Dennis, Nicolò Giacomin & Lucia Calfapietra, Lauren Hom, Lalalimola, Mick Marston, Jess Matthews, Chris Robertson, Marie Simpson, Alice Stevenson, Yulia Vysotskaya.

ISBN: 978 1 4889 0047 1

Printed and bound in China

CONTENTS

The wheels on the bus go round and round,
Round and round, round and round,
The wheels on the bus go round and round,
All through the town.

The door on the bus goes open and shut...

The wipers on the bus go swish, swish, swish...

The driver on the bus says 'Move on back...'

The people on the bus go up and down...

The babies on the bus go 'Wah, wah, wah...'

The mothers on the bus go 'Shh, shh, shh...'

Round and round the garden,
Like a teddy bear.
One step, two steps,
Tickle you under there!

THIS IS THE WAY THE *Ladies* RIDE,

TRIPPETY-*tee*, TRIPPETY-*tee*!

THIS IS THE WAY THE LADIES RIDE,

Trippety~trippety~tee!

THIS IS THE WAY THE GENTLEMEN RIDE,

JIGGETY-JOG, JIGGETY-JOG!

THIS IS THE *way* THE GENTLEMEN *ride*,

Jiggety-jiggety-jog!

THIS IS THE WAY THE
FARMERS RIDE,
HOBBLEDY-HOY, HOBBLEDY-HOY
THIS IS THE WAY THE FARMERS RIDE
HOBBLEDY·HOBBLEDY HOY!

THIS IS THE WAY
THE HUNTERS RIDE,
GALLOPY-GALLOP, GALLOPY-GALLOP!
THIS IS THE WAY THE hunters RIDE,
GALLOPY-GALLOPY-GALLOP
AND DOWN INTO THE DITCH!

Incy Wincy Spider
Climbed up the water spout.
Down came the rain
And washed poor Incy out.

Out came the sunshine
And dried up all the rain,
And Incy Wincy Spider
Climbed up the spout again.

Two fat gentlemen met in a lane,
Bowed most politely, bowed once again.
How do you do? How do you do?
How do you do again?

Two thin ladies
met in a lane…

Two tall policemen met in a lane…

Two little schoolboys met in a lane…

Two little babies met in a lane…

END OF ROAD

Five fat sausages
frying in a pan
One went POP!
And then it went BANG!

Four fat sausages
frying in a pan
One went POP!
And then it went BANG!

Three fat sausages
frying in a pan
One went POP!
And then it went BANG!

Two fat sausages frying in a pan
One went POP! And then it went BANG!

One fat sausage frying in a pan
One went POP! And then it went BANG!

And there were NO sausages left!

This little piggy went to market,
This little piggy stayed home;

This little piggy had roast beef,
This little piggy had none;

And this little piggy cried, 'Wee-wee-wee!'
All the way home.

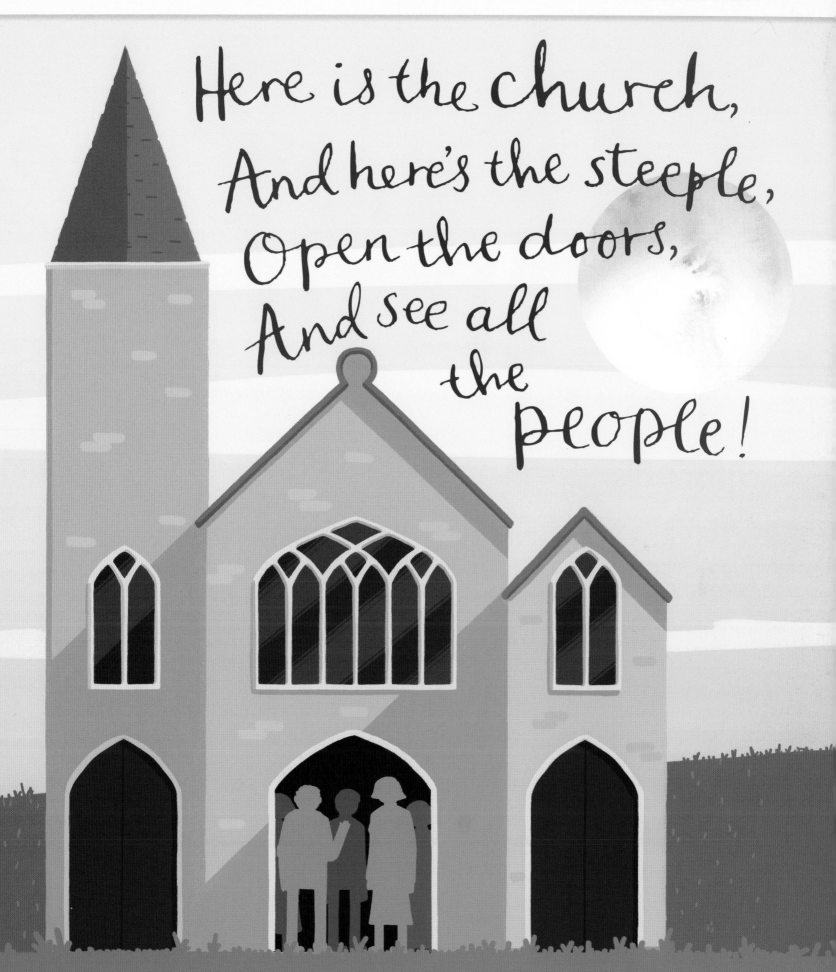

Pat-a-cake, pat-a-cake, baker's man.
Bake me a cake as fast as you can;
Pat it and prick it and mark it with B,
Put it in the oven for baby and me.

WHERE IS THUMBKIN?
WHERE IS THUMBKIN?
HERE I AM! HERE I AM!
How are you today, sir?
VERY WELL, I THANK YOU.
RUN AWAY. RUN AWAY.

WHERE
IS POINTER? (x2)
HERE I AM! HERE I AM!
HOW ARE YOU TODAY, SIR?
VERY WELL, I THANK YOU.
RUN AWAY. (x2)

Where is Tallman? (x2)
HERE I AM! (x2)
HOW ARE YOU TODAY, SIR?
very well, I thank you.
= RUN AWAY. (x2)

WHERE IS RINGMAN? (x2)
HERE I AM! (x2)
How are you today, sir?
VERY WELL, I THANK YOU.
RUN AWAY. RUN AWAY.

WHERE IS PINKIE? (x2)
HERE I AM! (x2)
HOW ARE YOU TODAY, SIR?
VERY WELL, I THANK YOU.
RUN AWAY. RUN AWAY.

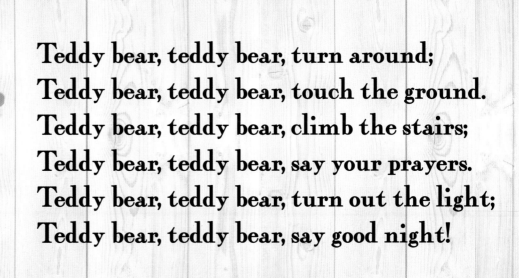

Teddy bear, teddy bear, turn around;
Teddy bear, teddy bear, touch the ground.
Teddy bear, teddy bear, climb the stairs;
Teddy bear, teddy bear, say your prayers.
Teddy bear, teddy bear, turn out the light;
Teddy bear, teddy bear, say good night!

TWO LITTLE DICKY BIRDS,
Sitting on a wall;
ONE NAMED PETER,
ONE NAMED PAUL.

Fly away PETER!
FLY AWAY Paul!
COME BACK PETER!
COME BACK PAUL!

Miss Polly had a dolly who was sick, sick, sick,
So she called for the doctor to come quick, quick, quick.
The doctor came with his bag and his hat,
And he knocked at the door with a rat-a-tat-tat!

He looked at the dolly and he shook his head,
And he said 'Miss Polly, put her straight to bed!'
He wrote on a paper for a pill, pill, pill,
'I'll be back in the morning with my bill, bill, bill.'

I'm a little teapot, short and stout,
Here is my handle, here is my spout.
When I get all steamed up, hear me shout,
Tip me over and pour me out!

I have ten little fingers,
And they all belong to me.
I can make them do things,
Would you like to see?

I can shut them up tight,
Or open them wide.
I can put them together,
Or make them all hide.

I can make them jump high,
I can make them go low.
I can fold them up quietly,
And hold them just so.

Here is the beehive,
But where are the bees?
Hidden away,
Where nobody sees.
Watch and you'll see them
Come out of the hive.
One, two, three, four, five.
Bzzzzzzzz!

Action Instructions

Round and Round the Garden (page 6)

(circle finger around child's palm) — Round and round the garden, Like a teddy bear.
(walk your fingers up child's arm) — One step, two steps,
(tickle under arm or chin) — Tickle you under there!

This Little Piggy (page 16)

(touch each of child's toes in turn with each line) — This little piggy went to market, This little piggy stayed home; This little piggy had roast beef, This little piggy had none;
(walk fingers up child's leg) — And this little piggy cried, 'Wee-wee-wee!'
(tickle belly or under arm) — All the way home.

I'm a Little Teapot (page 28)

(stand straight) — I'm a little teapot, short and stout,
(put hand on hip for handle) — Here is my handle,
(put out bent arm for spout) — here is my spout,
(tilt body to the spout side to pour tea) — When I get all steamed up, hear me shout, Tip me over and pour me out!

Incy Wincy Spider (page 10)

(alternately touch thumb of one hand to little finger of other) — Incy Wincy Spider, Climbed up the water spout.
(raise hands and wiggle fingers as you lower hands) — Down came the rain
(sweep hands from side to side) — And washed poor Incy out.
(raise hands and sweep side to side) — Out came the sunshine
(raise hands and wiggle fingers) — And dried up all the rain,
(repeat action for first line) — And Incy Wincy Spider, Climbed up the spout again.

Pat-a-Cake (page 20)

(clap hands in time with rhyme of rhyme) — Pat-a-cake, pat-a-cake, baker's man. Bake me a cake as fast as you can;
(trace B on palm) — Pat it and prick it and mark it with B,
(extend both hands) — Put it in the oven
(point to baby and self) — for baby and me.

Two Fat Gentlemen (page 12)

(hold up thumbs/forefinger/middle finger/ring finger/little finger facing each other) — Two fat gentlemen / ladies / policemen / schoolboys / babies met in a lane,
(bow fingers towards each other twice) — Bowed most politely, bowed once again.
(bow one finger towards the other) — How do you do?
(bow the other one finger towards the other) — How do you do?
(bow fingers towards each other) — How do you do again?

Where Is Thumbkin? (page 22)

(place hands behind back) — Where is Thumbkin / Pointer/ Tallman / Ringman / Pinkie? (x2)
(bring right hand to front, with thumb/forefinger/middle finger/ring finger/little finger up) — Here I am!
(do the same with the left hand) — Here I am!
(wiggle right thumb or finger) — How are you today, sir?
(wiggle left thumb or finger) — Very well, I thank you.
(place right hand behind back) — Run away.
(place left hand behind back) — Run away.

Two Little Dicky Birds (page 26)

(raise forefinger of each hand) — Two little dicky birds, Sitting on a wall;
(wiggle one figner) — One named Peter,
(wiggle other finger) — One named Paul.
(place one hand behind back) — Fly away Peter!
(place other hand behind back) — Fly away Paul!
(bring back one hand with forefinger raised) — Come back, Peter!
(bring back other hand with forefinger raised) — Come back, Paul!

Here Is the Beehive (page 31)

(hold up fist) — Here is the beehive, But where are the bees? Hidden away, Where nobody sees. Watch and you'll see them, Come out of the hive.
(count out fingers one at a time) — One, two, three, four, five.
(wiggle fingers) — Bzzzzzzzz

Here Is the Church (page 19)

(fold hands with fingers crossed inside and thumbs together pointing up) — Here is the church,
(raise both forefingers and create a point) — And here's the steeple,
(open thumbs up) — Open the doors,
(turn hands around and wiggle crossed fingers) — And see all the people!

This Is the Way the Ladies Ride (page 8)

(place child on knee facing you, bounce gently) — This is the way the ladies ride...
(bounce child a little faster but still gently) — This is the way the gentlemen ride...
(bounce child faster and a little higher) — This is the way the farmers ride...
(bounce child higher and faster) — This is the way the hunters ride...
(lift child up in the air) — And down into the ditch!

Miss Polly Had a Dolly (page 27)

(hold arms as if holding a baby and rock) — Miss Polly had a dolly who was sick, sick, sick,
(place hand to ear like phone and beckon finger) — So she called for the doctor to come quick, quick, quick.
(raise one hand as if holding a bag, and touch other to head) — The doctor came with his bag and his hat,
(knocking on door motion) — And he knocked at the door with a rat-a-tat-tat.
(shake head) — He looked at the dolly and he shook his head,
(shake finger as if scolding) — And he said 'Miss Polly, put her straight to bed!'
(pretend to write on palm with pencil) — He wrote on a paper for a pill, pill, pill,
(hold out paper) — 'I'll be back in the morning with my bill, bill, bill.'

Five Fat Sausages (page 14)

(hold up five/four/three/two/one fingers and move in a sizzling motion) — Five/Four/Three/Two/One fat sausages frying in a pan,
(pop cheek with finger) — One went pop!
(clap hands loudly) — And then it went BANG!...
(hold up closed fist) — And there were NO sausages left!

Ten Little Fingers (page 30)

(hold up 10 fingers) — I have ten little fingers,
(point to self) — And they all belong to me.
(wiggle fingers) — I can make them do things, Would you like to see?
(make fist) — I can shut them up tight,
(open hands) — Or open them wide.
(place palms together) — I can put them together,
(put hands behind back) — Or make them all hide.
(raise hands over head) — I can make them jump high,
(touch floor) — I can make them go low.
(fold hands in lap) — I can fold them up quietly, And hold them just so.

Teddy Bear, Teddy Bear (page 24)

(turn in circle) — Teddy bear, teddy bear, turn around;
(touch floor) — Teddy bear, teddy bear, touch the ground.
(act climbing stairs) — Teddy bear, teddy bear, climb the stairs;
(put hands together like praying) — Teddy bear, teddy bear, say your prayers.
(act blowing out candle) — Teddy bear, teddy bear, turn out the light;
(rest head on hand and close eyes) — Teddy bear, teddy bear, say good night!

The Wheels on the Bus (page 4)

(turn hands around each other) — The wheels on the bus go round and round...
(open hands and clap them together) — The door on the bus goes open and shut...
(swish arms back and forth like wipers) — The wipers on the bus go swish, swish, swish...
(point over shoulder with thumb) — The driver on the bus says 'Move on back....'
(sit up and down) — The people on the bus go up and down...
(rub eyes as though crying) — The babies on the bus go 'Wah, wah, wah...'
(put forefinger to mouth) — The mothers on the bus go 'Shh, shh, shh...'